It is no secret that Anansi the spider man allows his greed and selfishness to get the better of him, attracting trouble like bees to a honey-pot. He is also a coward, and when there's trouble he often escapes by changing from man to spider and scurrying away. But when he decides to use his own cleverness and trickster skills he can gain anything, from a cow to the ultimate prize of the Tiger Stories.

There are many different versions of Anansi's stories, originating in Ghana and spreading to the Caribbean, but this version from Jamaica is the one I have particularly enjoyed, and would like to share with you now.

In memory of my Father
Gerald Bancroft Bent

DUTTON

Published by the Penguin Group
Penguin Books Ltd, 27 Wrights Lane, London W8 5TZ, England
Penguin Books USA Inc., 375 Hudson Street, New York, New York 10014, USA
Penguin Books Australia Ltd, Ringwood, Victoria, Australia
Penguin Books Canada Ltd, 10 Alcorn Avenue, Toronto, Ontario, Canada M4V 3B2
Penguin Books (NZ) Ltd, 182–190 Wairau Road, Auckland 10, New Zealand

Penguin Books Ltd, Registered Offices: Harmondsworth, Middlesex, England

First published 1996
1 3 5 7 9 10 8 6 4 2

Copyright © Jenny Bent, 1996

The moral right of the author/illustrator has been asserted

Filmset in Monotype Baskerville

PRINTED IN BELGIUM BY

proost
INTERNATIONAL BOOK PRODUCTION

A CIP catalogue record for this book is available from the British Library
ISBN 0-525-69041-7

FOLK TALES OF THE WORLD

A CARIBBEAN FOLK TALE

HOW ANANSI CAPTURED TIGER'S STORIES

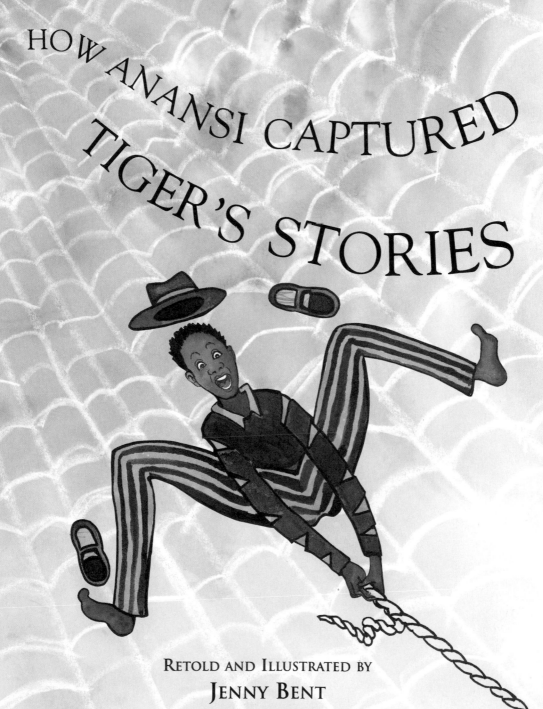

RETOLD AND ILLUSTRATED BY
JENNY BENT

DUTTON

Many years ago, long before Lion was King of the Jungle, Tiger ruled over the animals. He was very strong and powerful and greatly feared – he was the type of big cat who had many things named after him.

The bright orange lily was called the tiger-lily. The moth, with big broad stripes on its wings, was called the tiger-moth. And the magical stories the jungle animals told at evening were called the Tiger Stories.

As for Anansi the spider man, nothing was named after him. He was such a coward that when lightning flashed in the skies he changed from man to spider and hid under a rock. But Anansi loved the Tiger Stories and wanted them to be named after him.

One day Anansi decided to ask
Tiger for the Stories.

He bowed low, and begged
quite pitifully,

'I . . . I . . . would . . . like the
Tiger stories to be called the
Anansi Stories. Please.'

This made Tiger very angry, as
he loved his Stories more than
anything else in the world. But as
king and ruler he had to be fair.
Even if he didn't want to be.

Tiger gave the matter some thought.

'If you want my beloved stories you will have to work for them,' he growled. 'I will set you two tasks. In one week you must bring me a gourd-jar full of live bees, and capture Python Snake,' said Tiger, majestically lifting his right paw. 'You must succeed in both tasks, and only then shall I make it known that my prized Tiger Stories will become the Anansi Tales.'

'Yes, mighty Tiger,' whispered Anansi.

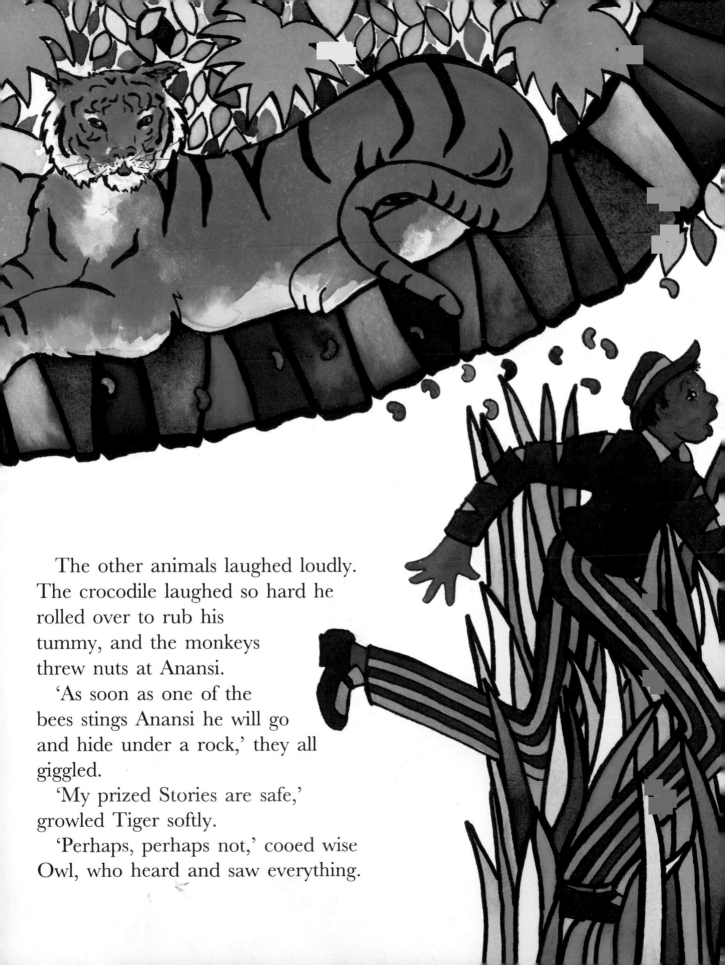

The other animals laughed loudly. The crocodile laughed so hard he rolled over to rub his tummy, and the monkeys threw nuts at Anansi.

'As soon as one of the bees stings Anansi he will go and hide under a rock,' they all giggled.

'My prized Stories are safe,' growled Tiger softly.

'Perhaps, perhaps not,' cooed wise Owl, who heard and saw everything.

The next day, Anansi left home smiling to himself.
He had a large gourd-jar tucked under his arm. As he
walked through the forest he kept on mumbling to
himself, 'How many will fit inside this gourd-jar? How
many will fit inside?'

The giraffe stooped his long neck nearer to listen.
'Why are you talking to yourself, Anansi?'

But Anansi would not say. Many other animals
asked but they too got no reply.

Finally, the Queen Bee flew up to Anansi.

'What on earth are you gibbering to yourself?' she
buzzed.

'Oh, Queen Bee, Tiger told me to find out how many bees can fit snugly in this gourd-jar,' Anansi replied.

Hot gossip travels even faster than a loud sneeze in the jungle, but even so Queen Bee did not yet know the true story.

'How silly,' she buzzed impatiently.

'I couldn't agree more,' Anansi humbly replied, 'but can you help me?'

'Not now. I haven't got the time. I'm off to join my other worker bees to complete a good day's work.'

And she buzzed off without uttering another word.

At the end of the day the Queen led her worker bees back to their hive. She saw Anansi in the same spot still miserably muttering to himself.

'Haven't you solved your problem yet?'

'No, ma'am,' said Anansi sadly.

'Why don't you measure the size of one of my bees and multiply it until you get the right answer?' said Queen Bee.

But I'm no good at maths,' replied Anansi.

'Then I have another idea. I shall get all my bees to fly into the jar, and you can count them that way . . . you can count can't you?' she buzzed doubtfully.

'Oh yes, yes, I can count if you all fly in very slowly,' said Anansi happily.

Queen Bee led the way, commanding all the other bees to follow. Anansi held out his jar and counted 'One, two, three, four, five . . . thirty . . . forty . . . fifty . . . HALF FULL one hundred and one . . . two . . . three . . . ALMOST FULL . . . ' And as the very last bee squeezed into the jar 'PLENTY FULL!'

Anansi hurriedly placed the lid on the jar and trapped all the angry bees inside. Then he rushed back to find Tiger.

'Here is the gourd-jar full of bees, O Tiger,' beamed Anansi, very pleased with himself.

Tiger had heard that Anansi had gone crazy, talking to himself, so you can imagine how shocked he was to see Anansi return, with a jar stuffed full of bees.

'But you haven't been stung even once!' protested Tiger.

'Anyway, I . . . I don't believe you!'

'Shall I open up the jar for you to have a look?' asked Anansi.

'NO, NO . . .' chorused all the animals, who had already heard the bees buzzing angrily, 'it's all right. We believe you!'

'Good,' said Anansi. 'Then I'm off to complete my second task.'

'He will never catch Python Snake,' Tiger growled, a little worried now.

'Who-oo-oo can tell,' cooed Owl. 'Let's wait and see.'

Anansi quite honestly didn't have a clue how to capture the giant Python Snake. But first he had to solve another problem, one he was definitely not looking forward to – setting free a whole swarm of angry bees. Carefully, he took the lid from the gourd-jar, then ran for his life. But the bees were so tired from buzzing loudly and stomping their little feet on the walls of the jar, none of them had the energy to fly after Anansi and give him a good stinging for tricking them.

All that night Anansi tossed and turned as he thought about how to catch Python Snake. Early the next day Anansi left his home with a plan.

'I am going to catch Python Snake,' he whistled confidently. Anansi knew all Python Snake's habits. He knew what he ate, where he slept and all the best areas he slithered in.

He built a cage from bamboo sticks in Python Snake's favourite place and put a large, ripe, juicy mango fruit inside.

Then he sat and waited for Python Snake. But Python Snake was too quick. He slid into the cage, swallowed the mango and slid out again, as quick as you could blink an eye. Poor Anansi had not only failed to capture Python Snake, he had also lost his juicy mango.

The next day, Anansi left home with a new
plan. 'I am going to catch Python Snake,' he whistled.
But this time there was doubt in his voice. Anansi made
another trap, using a long piece of rope covered with leaves
and an egg on top. Then he sat and waited patiently until
Python Snake slithered by. Python Snake snatched the egg
into his mouth and gulped it down. As quick as a flash,
Anansi pulled the rope and the noose tightened itself
around Python Snake's head. But Python Snake was so big
he didn't even notice and dragged Anansi bumpety-bump
all the way home.

'No way can I catch Python,' groaned Anansi when he
finally let go of the rope, rubbing his battered and bruised
bottom. 'No way can I catch Snake.'

The week was almost at an
end, and still Anansi had failed
to capture Python Snake.
Then he saw Python Snake by
the river and another idea
came to him. A little later
Python Snake heard two voices
arguing behind some bushes.

'The mighty Python Snake is much longer than that!'

'Of course he isn't!'

'Yes, he is!'

'No, he isn't!'

Python Snake was curious and went to see what was happening.
He found Anansi on his own.

'Who were you talking to . . . what were you ssssaying about
me?' he asked Anansi.

'Oh, I was arguing with someone who was very silly,' replied Anansi. 'He said that you are much shorter than this stick, but you're not, are you?'

'Of coursssse not! I'm much longer than thissss ssstick,' hissed Python Snake, and without being asked, he slapped his whole body against the long stick.

'Keep still!' ordered Anansi. 'If you slither about, how can I be sure that when I run up to your head, you won't crawl up the stick, and when I go down to see where your tail is you won't wriggle down?'

'ARE YOU SSSSAYING I'M A CHEAT?' thundered Python Snake.

'No, but my friend will when I tell him,' said Anansi. Let me tie you to the stick with reeds from the river, then it will solve our problem.'

Python Snake, eager to prove how long he was, agreed, and Anansi tied him to the stick.

Anansi had finally captured Python Snake.

Proudly, Anansi took Python Snake to Tiger. From that day he gained the praise of the other animals, and also the prized Tiger Stories which are now called the Anansi Tales . . . But to this day Anansi has always carefully avoided the bees and Python Snake, who were all tricked by the trickiest trickster of them all.